for my second daughter

Isabella Felicity Laura

THE
LANGUAGE
OF FLOWERS

compiled and illustrated by Helen Williams

E. P. DUTTON · NEW YORK

Child do you love the flower
Ashine with colour and dew
Lighting its transient hour?
    So I love you.

'Envoy,' WALTER DE LA MARE
from *Songs of Childhood*

SNOWDROP

HOPE

The snowdrop, in purest white array
First rears its head on Candlemas Day.

ANON.

PRIMROSE

EARLY YOUTH

And in dark woods the wandering little one
May find a primrose.

HARTLEY COLERIDGE

POPPY

EXTRAVAGANCE

Just simply alive
Both of us, I
And the poppy.

ISSA

IRIS

MESSAGE

A day of rain,
Somebody passes my gate
with irises.

SHINTOKU

LOVE-IN-A-MIST

PERPLEXITY

'Bunches of grapes,' says Timothy
'Pomegranates pink,' says Elaine,
'A junket of cream and a cranberry tart
For me,' says Jane.

'Love-in-a-mist,' says Timothy,
'Primroses pale,' says Elaine
'A nosegay of pinks and mignonette
For me,' says Jane.

'Bunches of Grapes,' WALTER DE LA MARE
from *Songs of Childhood*

FORGET-ME-NOT

DO NOT FORGET ME

Buttercup, Poppy, Forget-me-not –
These three bloomed in a garden spot;
And once, all merry with song and play,
A little one heard three voices say:
"Shine and shadow, summer and spring,
O thou child with the tangled hair
And laughing eyes! We three shall bring
Each an offering passing fair."
The little one did not understand,
But they bent and kissed the dimpled hand.

'Buttercup, Poppy, Forget-me-not,'
EUGENE FIELD from *Poems of Childhood*

PINK

BOLDNESS

The Pink can no one justly slight
The gardener's favourite flower.

GOETHE

PEONY

SHAME · BASHFULNESS

"The peony was as big as this"
Says the little girl
Opening her arms.

ISSA

PANSY

YOU OCCUPY MY THOUGHTS

While pansies sunward look,
        that glorious light
With gentle beams entering
        their purple bowers
Sheds there his love and heat
        and fair to sight
Prints his bright form
        within their golden flowers

PHINEAS FLETCHER

HONEYSUCKLE

DEVOTED AFFECTION

What brings the sea-wind so far inland?
It is a memory of honeysuckle
Which nullifies the years between
This garden and those ragged hedges,
Teasing the nostrils, moistening the eyes,
Confronting me with you and you with me.

'Honeysuckle Smell,' J A M E S R E E V E S from *Collected Poems*

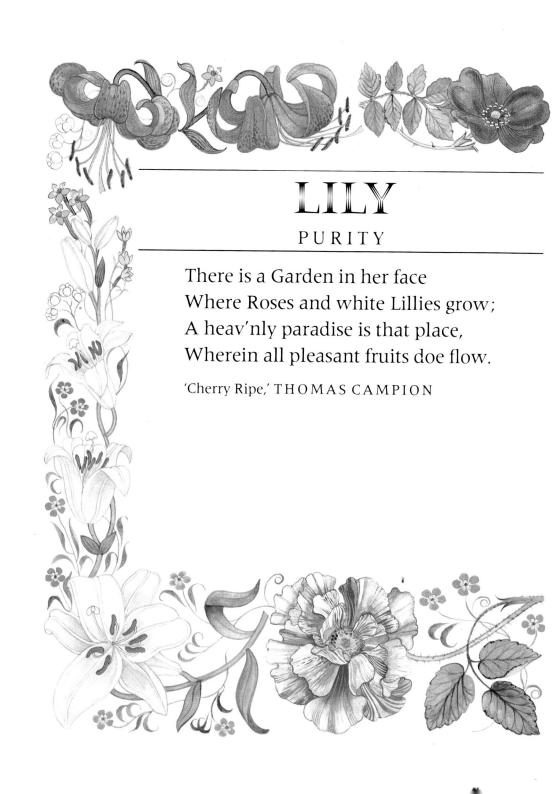

LILY

PURITY

There is a Garden in her face
Where Roses and white Lillies grow;
A heav'nly paradise is that place,
Wherein all pleasant fruits doe flow.

'Cherry Ripe,' THOMAS CAMPION

ROSE

LOVE

Queen rose of the rosebud garden of girls
Come hither, the dances are done,
In gloss of satin and glimmer of pearls,
Queen lily and rose in one,
Shine out, little head, sunning over with curls,
To the flowers, and be their sun.

'Come into the Garden Maud,' ALFRED TENNYSON

ANEMONE
FORSAKEN

I send a garland to my love
Which with my own hands I wove
Rose and Lily here there be
Twined with cool anemone.

RUFINUS

JASMINE

ATTACHMENT

My slight and slender jasmine-tree,
That bloomest on my border tower
Thou art more dearly loved by me
Than all the wealth of fairy bower.

LORD MORPETH

LILY-OF-THE-VALLEY

RETURN OF HAPPINESS

. . . To the Curious eye
A little monitor presents her page
Of choice instruction, with her snowy bells
The lily of the vale . . .

'The Lily-of-the-Valley,' JAMES HURDIS

SWEET WILLIAM

GALLANTRY

Soon shall we have gold-dusted snapdragon,
Sweet William with its homely cottage smell,
And Stocks in fragrant blow . . .

'Thyrsis,' MATTHEW ARNOLD

DAISY

INNOCENCE

In the scented bud of the morning – O
When the windy grass went rippling far,
I saw my dear one walking slow,
In the field where the daisies are.

A lark sang up from the breezy land
A lark sang down from a cloud afar
And she and I went hand in hand
In the field where the daisies are.

'The Daisies' JAMES STEPHENS

LILAC

FIRST EMOTIONS OF LOVE

Just now the lilac is in bloom
All before my little room,
And in my flower-beds, I think
Smile the carnation and the pink,
And down the borders well I know
The poppy and the pansy blow . . .

'The Old Vicarage, Grantchester,' RUPERT B·ROOKE

DAFFODIL

REGARD

When all at once I saw a crowd
A host, of golden daffodils;
Beside the lake, beneath the trees,
Fluttering and dancing in the breeze.

'Daffodils,' WILLIAM WORDSWORTH

TULIP

FAME

Yet, rich as morn of many hue,
When flashing clouds through darkness strike,
The Tulip's petals shine like dew,
All beautiful, yet none alike.

MONTGOMERY

VIOLET

MODESTY

To pluck it is a pity
To leave it is a pity
Ah, this violet!

NAOJO

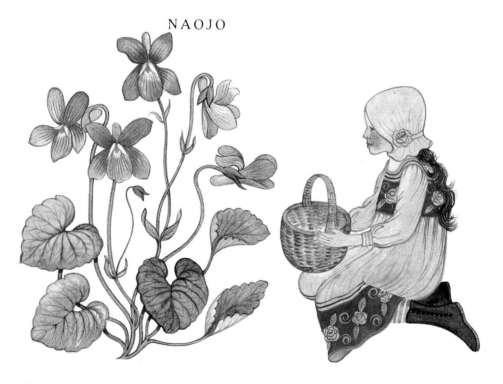

MORNING GLORY
AFFECTATION

I am one
Who eats his breakfast
Gazing at the morning-glories.

BASHO

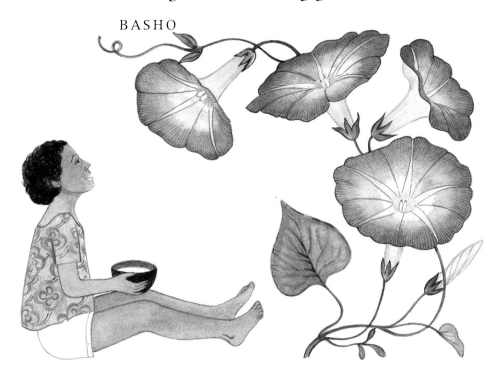

COLUMBINE

FOLLY

Tulips are faded. Honeysuckles still in beauty.
My Columbines are very beautiful.

GILBERT WHITE

HYACINTH

SPORT · PLAY

'Light-hearted I walked into the valley wood
In the time of hyacinths.'

'Conversation,' T.E. HULME

MICHAELMAS DAISY

FAREWELL

The full colour artwork is painted
in watercolour and gouache
using very fine sable brushes
on Saunders HP 90lb/140lb paper.